My Wonderful Day

by Alan Ayckbourn

CW00553073

A SAMUEL FRENCH ACTING EDITION

SAMUEL FRENCH

FOUNDED 1830

NEW YORK HOLLYWOOD LONDON TORONTO

SAMUELFRENCH.COM

ISBN 978-0-573-69949-8   Printed in U.S.A.   #29743

MUSIC USE NOTE

Licensees are solely responsible for obtaining formal written permission from copyright owners to use copyrighted music in the performance of this play and are strongly cautioned to do so. If no such permission is obtained by the licensee, then the licensee must use only original music that the licensee owns and controls. Licensees are solely responsible and liable for all music clearances and shall indemnify the copyright owners of the play and their licensing agent, Samuel French, Inc., against any costs, expenses, losses and liabilities arising from the use of music by licensees.

IMPORTANT BILLING AND CREDIT
REQUIREMENTS

All producers of *MY WONDERFUL DAY must* give credit to the Author of the Play in all programs distributed in connection with performances of the Play, and in all instances in which the title of the Play appears for the purposes of advertising, publicizing or otherwise exploiting the Play and/ or a production. The name of the Author *must* appear on a separate line on which no other name appears, immediately following the title and *must* appear in size of type not less than fifty percent of the size of the title type.

MY WONDERFUL DAY was first presented at the Stephen Joseph Theatre, Scarborough on October 13, 2009. The performance was directed by Alan Ayckbourn, with sets by Roger Glossop, and lighting by Mick Hughes. The cast was as follows:

KEVIN	Terence Booth
LAVERNE	Petra Letang
WINNIE	Ayesha Antoine
TIFFANY	Ruth Gibson
JOSH	Paul Kemp
PAULA	Alexandra Mathie

It was subsequently presented at 59E59 Theaters, New York, on November 11th with the same cast. A UK tour followed in January 2010.

CHARACTERS

WINNIE (WINONA) BARNSTAIRS - nearly 9
LAVERNE BARNSTAIRS - her mother, late 20s/early 30s
THE MAN (KEVIN TATE) - 40s
PAULA - his wife, late 30s
TIFFANY - the secretary, 20s
JOSH - the friend, 40s

SETTING

The action takes place in and around Kevin Tate's house in North London on a Tuesday in November.

TIME

The present.

AUTHOR'S NOTES

It is appreciated that one of the difficulties of this play is in casting Winnie the right age. Either she needs to be played by a young actor of a similar age with all the ensuing legal and logistical problems which casting an under-age performer entails or the role may be played by a slightly older actor who is able to create a truthful and credible impression of the character's age. This, after all, is theatre! In either case, it is vital that the role is not in any way "up-aged". Winnie is a child and this play is told through a child's eyes.

The partial downstairs areas of a modern town house belonging to the Man. A Tuesday in November.

What we see is perceived through the eyes of a nine-year old girl, **Winnie (Winona) Barnstairs,** *thus each area is lit as she enters it and correspondingly darkens as she leaves.*

Sometimes it will be part of the hall/living room, especially the immediate area around the sofa and coffee table. This hall is the carpeted, open plan ground floor hub of the house. Leading off it, are ways to the front door, the stairs, the office and the kitchen. Other areas skeletally represented are the office also carpeted, represented by (at least) an easy chair, a small desk and a swivel desk chair and the kitchen, represented by a table with a minimum of three chairs around it and a separate easy chair, possibly a modern style rocker.

8.30 a.m.

It starts in black-out. The house doorbell sounds. After a moment, November morning light comes up on the hall area through slatted blinds. It is still comparatively early.

The **Man** *is leading* **Laverne** *and* **Winnie** *from the front door where he has just let them in. He is about forty, still in his shortie dressing-gown and barefoot having recently got out of bed. He is unshaven and tousled and appears to have had a rough night. Laverne is late twenties, second generation Afro-Caribbean south London and heavily pregnant. With her is her daughter,* **Winnie,** *nearly nine years old, a silent watchful child. She carries her school bag.*

Throughout this next exchange, the **Man** *gives both of them barely a glance, particularly* **Winnie** *whom he ignores completely. He is uneasy with children.*

Laverne. *(as they enter)* … I'm so sorry, Mr Tate, I arranged all this with Mrs Tate, you see. Last Friday. She kindly agreed I could come and clean this Tuesday instead of tomorrow. Wednesday, I have this doctor's appointment, you see …

Man. *(only half listening)* … yeah … yeah … that's OK. No problems.

He moves away from them to the kitchen and glances in.

Laverne. … I did warn Mrs Tate on Friday that I couldn't come Wednesday, that I'd have to come Tuesday. I mean, I did offer her Thursday or even possibly Monday. But Mrs Tate seemed to think Tuesday would be more convenient …

Man. *(calling into the kitchen)* Paula!

Laverne. … I mean, it's just for my regular check up. But I daren't miss it. They don't like it if you miss it …

Man. *(frowning)* … right, right … *(calling, louder)* Paula!

Contenting himself there is no one there he leaves the kitchen, and moves to the office.

Laverne. *(continuing regardless, following behind him)* … it's only my regular Wednesday check, you see. I mean, I did try having them move it to Thursday but they were adamant for Wednesday and you don't like to miss them, do you? And then this morning, I had to phone Mrs Tate — oh, an hour ago, it must have been — I had to ring her on her mobile … I couldn't get no reply from this number …

Man. … no … *(now in the office doorway, calling:)* Paulie!

Laverne. … just to warn her I'd be bringing Winnie with me as well 'cause she was feeling little bit under the weather and she wasn't really up to going to her school. Nothing serious, a little bit throaty, weren't you, darling…? Bit throaty, aren't you …?

Winnie *nods.*

Man. Oh, dear… *(He returns finally to the hall.)* Paulie! *(muttering)* It's unbelievable …!

Laverne. *(still trailing behind him with* **Winnie***)* … and Mrs Tate ever so kindly said it would be all right if I was to bring Winnie with me just for an hour or so, while I did round. Just while I was working …

Man. *(moving briskly towards the front door and yelling)* PAUL-IE! *(muttering)* I don't believe this …!

Laverne. Winnie's promised me she's going to sit nice and quiet, aren't you, Winnie?

Winnie *nods.*

She's got her books and her homework, she's promised me she won't be in anyone's way. It'll be all right for her to sit here on the sofa here …?

Man. What time is it?

Laverne. Just gone eight-thirty.

Man. *(going up the stairs)* I must get dressed.

Laverne. She's not here then?

Man. Who?

Laverne. Mrs Tate?

Man. Apparently not.

Laverne. Oh. Must have gone to work, then.

Man. So it would appear ...

The **Man** *goes off upstairs.*

Laverne. *(after him)* Winnie's promised she'll be very quiet

———

Upstairs, a door slams.

 (Tailing off) — she won't disturb you ... *(turning her attention to* **Winnie***)* Now, quiet as a mouse, understand? You finish that homework first, all right? Before you do anything else. You write your essay you should have done last night.

Laverne *busies herself removing both their coats, scarves, etc.* **Winnie** *sits herself on the sofa. She starts to unpack her school bag producing, amongst other things, an exercise book and various pens and pencils.*

Remember what Mrs Crackle told you to do, don't you? You're to write about "My Wonderful Day". So you write that at the top of the page first — My Wonderful Day …

Winnie. I know …

Laverne. "My Wonderful Day by Winnie Barnstairs".

Winnie. Mum …!

Laverne. Tell you what, you could write it about today, couldn't you? Instead of yesterday? Today, it might be more interesting than yesterday. You could start by saying how we came here on the bus …

Winnie. *(squirming)* Mum …

Laverne. Besides, you didn't do nothing yesterday except lie on your bed …

Winnie. I was ill, wasn't I?

Laverne. … and then you could write how we just met Mr Tate …

Winnie. Mum, I can do it! Let me do it.

Laverne. I'm just starting you off …

Winnie. I'm all right, leave me, I can do it …

Laverne. All right, all right! I'm only helping … Use the pencil. Don't use the pen! You'll get ink on her sofa.

Winnie. I've got to use the pen …

Laverne. She thinks the world of this sofa …

Winnie. … we're not allowed to use pencil …

Laverne. … you can use pencil …

Winnie. I've got to write in pen. Mrs Crackle says we have to use pen …

Laverne. Yes, well. Just don't get ink on their sofa, will you? Mrs Tate's pride and joy this sofa …

Winnie. I won't.

Laverne. I know you and pens. All over your sheets, wasn't it? Be careful, that's all.

Laverne *goes off to hang up their coats by the front door.*

Winnie *pulls a face and then starts to write. Upstairs, footsteps are heard from the bedroom which causes her to look up briefly.*

Laverne *returns.*

Oh, isn't this a beautiful house, Winnie? Didn't I tell you, it was beautiful? Isn't it gorgeous?

Winnie. *(absorbed)* Yes.

Laverne. She's got lovely taste, Mrs Tate. Lovely little touches. You should see the bedrooms … Maybe one day, darling, we'll live somewhere like this, won't we? If I can get a nice job and if your dad starts sending the money again. Well, maybe not quite as big a place as this. But somewhere smaller, nice and cosy — tasteful — just you and me — no, well, three of us by then, won't there be? You, me, and your baby brother.

Winnie. *(staring at her mother's bump apprehensively)* Yeah …
Laverne. And when we look out of our window, we'll be looking at this beautiful bluey-green sea and the sunshine and the palm trees. And maybe little white boats bobbing about. It won't be like this, will it? Looking at the road and the houses opposite. It'll be even nicer than this.
Winnie. *(muttering)* If we go.
Laverne. What?
Winnie . *(who's heard this a number of times)* We've got to get there first, haven't we?
Laverne. We're going to get there. Don't worry, Winnie. Soon as I've had this baby, we're off, girl. We're going, I promise you. Trust me.

Winnie *doesn't answer. During the next,* **Laverne** *changes out of her boots and into her work shoes. Because of her current state,* **Winnie** *has to help her mother.*

Winnie, I mean it, trust me. Trust your mum. I've promised you, haven't I? You know what I feel about promises, don't you? You know when I promise something, I always keep it, don't you?
Winnie. Sometimes you can't.
Laverne. Can't what?
Winnie. Keep them. Promises. Sometimes you can't keep them.
Laverne. If you can't keep them, you shouldn't make them. You should never make promises you can't keep, either.
Winnie. You promised Dad.
Laverne. What?
Winnie. *(tying* **Laverne**'s *laces)* When you married him. You promised Dad.
Laverne. Yes. Well. That was different. He promised me too, didn't he? Till he broke it.
Winnie. Yeah.
Laverne. I didn't break that one, he did. Anyway, we're not talking about him, not this morning. Don't get me started on him … He gets talked about enough as it is … I must get on. I'll start on the kitchen, I think …
Winnie. You just go carefully …
Laverne. I'm all right, I'm all right. I feel fine. Another ten days yet.

Winnie. After you nearly fell over. Mrs Copthorne said to be careful ——

Laverne. When I had you I was working right up till the day before you popped out almost ——

Winnie. That was different. You weren't doing all this cleaning then though, were you? Sitting behind a desk then.

Laverne. I was right as rain. Felt perfectly fine. Now, you just get on.

Laverne *makes a move towards the kitchen.* **Winnie** *shrugs and gives up. Her mother is impossible.*

Laverne *goes out briefly but returns almost at once, attempting to tie an apron, stretched impossibly tightly around her increased girth.*

Oy! Oy! Yes, Miss! Talking of promises ... what day is it today, then? *Quel jour est lui aujourd'hui?* Tuesday. *C'est mardi, n'est ce pas?* And what do we do every *mardi?*

Winnie. Oh, Mum ... No.

Laverne. Tuesday is French day. We practise our French today, don't we?

Winnie. I can't. Not here!

Laverne. Yes, you can.

Winnie. What about you?

Laverne. I'm working. There's an excuse for me. No excuse for you. Day off school.

Winnie. I'm ill.

Laverne. No, you're not.

Winnie. I got this terrible throat. I can't talk in French.

Laverne. You're not ill.

Winnie. I am ...

Laverne. *(still struggling to tie her apron)* Soon as we got on the bus, you forgot all about it.

Winnie. *(going to* **Laverne**'*s assistance)* I didn't want to go to school, I was worried about you.

Laverne. That's very kind of you. But you worry about me in French.

Winnie. I don't know how to say it.

Laverne. Well, look it up then. You've got your dictionary with you, haven't you? If you don't know a word for something, you look it up. That's the only way you learn,

Winnie. Soon as I'm done here, I'm switching to French as well. You know what we said. We'll learn together, won't we? That's what we agreed. We both promised. We'll be glad of it later. When we get there. Very few of them speak English there, you know. My grandmother, she couldn't speak a word of English — did you know that?

Winnie. Yeah, yeah. You told me.

Laverne. *(in rather dodgy French) Ah! Ah! Ah! En français s'il vous plaît, ma chérie.*

Winnie. *(only slightly better) Oui, Maman.*

Laverne. *Bien! Bien! Je retour bientôt. Attente là, ma fille.*

Winnie. *(wearily) Oui, Maman.*

Laverne *goes off to the kitchen.*

Winnie *stares after her.*

(to herself) She's mad! Mad! *(after a moment's consideration) Elle est fou. Ma mère est une loonie!*

Winnie *continues writing. This is the first of several occasions when we see her on her own. She concentrates on her essay, writing slowly and laboriously with her pen. She takes in events occurring around her without reaction or comment, only sneaking a covert glance when she thinks no one sees her, which in general they don't. As a result, she becomes the child in the corner whom no one notices.*

(To herself slowly, as she writes) My ... Wonderful ... Day ... by ... Winnie ...

9 a.m.

The **Man** *comes downstairs, now dressed. He is talking on his mobile.*

Hearing him, after a quick glance, **Winnie** *gets her head down and concentrates on her writing.*

Man. *(as he enters ... on the phone, not even glancing at* **Winnie***)* ... yes ... yes ... where are you at present, Tiffy? ... What, in her office? In my office? ... June's in there with you,

then? ... Is she listening? ... *(laughing sarcastically)* I bet ...
I bet she is ... no, no ... Paula's not here. Definitely. ... I
don't know, do I? ... I've tried it. Dozens of times. She's
not answering ... no. ... She talks to the bloody cleaning
woman, she refuses to talk to me. ... Look, we can't —
Listen, Tiffy darling, we can't — Look, come round here.
Hop in a taxi and come round here straight away. We
can't talk on the phone — not with you in the middle of
the office, can we? ... Not with June ear-wigging. ... No,
there's no one here at present ... nobody. ... Look, Tiffy,
just grab a taxi, darling. ... Oh, yes, has it? Has it? I'll be
keen to see that — see how that's turned out ... Yes. ...
Listen, grab a copy, bring it round with you, darling. We
can have a look at it here. ... Yes. See you, darling. Yes
see you soon, babe ... love you, precious. *(He rings off. To
himself)* Right, coffee, coffee, coffee ...

He goes off into the office, briefly.

Winnie *continues to write.*

(off, from the office) Oh, shit!

The **Man** *returns with an empty cona jug.*

(seeing **Winnie** *for the first time)* All right there, kid?
Winnie. *Oui, monsieur. Merci beaucoup.*

The **Man** *goes out to the kitchen, staring at Winnie, puzzled.*

Slight pause. **Winnie** *continues to write.*

Voices from the kitchen.

Laverne. *(off, from the kitchen)* ... oh, no, that's quite all
right, Mr Tate. You carry on in here.
Man. *(off, from the kitchen)* Won't be second, Mrs ... er ...
Just making some fresh coffee ...
Laverne. *(off)* Would you like me to make you some?
Man. *(off)* No, no. It's all right. I'm just topping up the
machine in the office ...
Laverne. *(off)* I could easily make you some. It's no trouble
...
Man. *(off)* No, no. I can manage, Mrs ...er ....

In a moment, the **Man** *returns from the kitchen with the jug now filled with water and a bag of fresh ground coffee. He goes off again to the office, whistling under his breath.*

Winnie *writes on. From the kitchen there is the sound of crockery clattering and cutlery clinking as* **Laverne** *tidies away. The house phone rings loudly. In the office, the* **Man** *answers it.*

(*off, on the phone in the office*) ... Hallo ... Brian, mate! ... how did it go then? ... yes ... yes ... no ... yes ... (*Bellowing with laughter*) ... She what? ... (*He laughs again at length*) ... She didn't? ... (*He gives another huge laugh. Whatever it is whoever she is did, it is evidently hilarious*) ... yep ... yep ... *fucking* hell! ... never ... fuck me — ! ... hang on a tick, Brian, just a tick ... Don't go away, I want to hear the rest of this ...

He laughs again. The office door is heard to close. The **Man***'s laugh is heard again faintly now, muffled. From time to time we hear his laugh again through the door.* **Winnie***, who has reacted to none of this, continues to write her essay, concentrating deeply on her task.*

After a moment, **Laverne** *returns from the kitchen in kitchen gloves.*

Laverne. All right, darling?
Winnie. Oui, Maman. Je suis très content.
Laverne. Good girl. Est ce que quelques choses que tu désire, chérie?
Winnie. Non. Rien, Maman, merci.
Laverne. (*inspecting Winnie's work*) Ah. Bon! C'est bon. Bravo!
Winnie. (*instinctively covering her work with her hand*) Merci, Maman.

Laverne *makes to move back to the kitchen then, seeing her bag where she left it stops, remembering something.*

Laverne. Ah, Winnie, ma chère. Ici.

Laverne *rummages in her bag and produces a crumpled travel leaflet. In the office, the* **Man** *laughs again.*

Winnie. Quoi?

Laverne. *(putting the leaflet next to Winnie)* Là. Regardez.
   Martinique.
Winnie. *(without great enthusiasm)* Ah. Oui.
Laverne. C'est belle, non?
Winnie. Oui.
Laverne. *(opening the leaflet)* Tu regarde. Les montagnes …
   les plages … les voitures … les — *(unsure of the word)* —
   les palm trees — les arbres de palmes — c'est très belle,
   non?
Winnie. *(trying her best)* Oui. C'est trop belle, Maman.

In the office, the **Man** *laughs again.*

Laverne. *(putting the leaflet down beside Winnie)* Ici. Là. Pour
   tu, ma chèrie.
Winnie. *(without touching it)* Merci, Maman.

Laverne *moves back towards the kitchen.*

Laverne. Cinq minutes. Je retourne. Bien?
Winnie. Bien.

   Laverne *goes.*

   (After a brief glance at the leaflet) Ma mère est completement
   weird.

9.45 a.m.

Winnie *puts down the leaflet and returns to her writing. In the office, the* **Man** *laughs again. A pause. The doorbell rings.* **Winnie**
ignores it. After a second, it rings again.

   Laverne *comes from the kitchen. As she does so, the office door
   opens briefly.*

Man. *(off)* Can someone get that?
Laverne. *(calling)* Yes, I'm going, I'm just going, Mr Tate.
   I'll get it.
Man. *(off, calling)* Probably be Miss Cavendish …

The office door closes again.

Laverne *goes out to the front door. In a moment she returns with* **Tiffany**, *smartly dressed for work, in her mid-twenties. She is holding the morning post which she's just picked up from the mat and a brown envelope containing a DVD which she has brought from the office.*

Laverne. *(as they enter)* Please come through. Mr Tate's just through here …

Tiffany. *(cheerfully)* Thanks. Hi, I'm Tiffany, by the way. Just in case you were wondering who you were letting through the door … I work with Mr Tate.

Laverne. How do you do. I'm Mrs — Laverne. Laverne Barnstairs. I'm the cleaner. Doing a little bit of cleaning for him.

Tiffany. Yah, jolly good. You carry on, don't let me interrupt. Through here is he?

Laverne. In the office, there. I think he's just on the phone, I think.

Another bellow of laughter from the office.

Tiffany. *(hearing this)* Yes, well, I'll — wait a — *(seeing Winnie for the first time)* — Oh, hallo. Who's this, then?

Laverne. This is my daughter.

Tiffany. Oh, isn't she pretty! Hallo, there! And what's your name?

Winnie *hesitates, uncertain how to reply.*

Laverne. Say hallo, Winnie.

Winnie. Bonjour, mam'selle.

Tiffany. *(enchanted)* Oh! *(to* **Laverne***)* Isn't that lovely? *(crouching down, to* **Winnie***)* What's your name, then?

Winnie. Je m'appelle Winnie, mam'selle.

Tiffany. Winnie! And how old are you, Winnie?

Winnie. J'ai neuf ans, mam'selle.

Laverne. Nine. She's nine next month.

Tiffany. Enchanting. Does she always speak in French?

Laverne. On Tuesdays, she does. I encourage her every Tuesday.

Tiffany. *(mystified)* Oh.

Laverne. We both do. *(to* **Winnie***)* Nous parlons le français toutes les mardis, n'est ce pas, ma petite?

Winnie. Oui, Maman. C'est vrai.

Laverne. We're not that good, but we're getting better, aren't we?

Tiffany. How brilliant. What a brilliant idea! Every Tuesday, you say?

Laverne. Every Tuesday, yes.

Tiffany. What do you speak on Wednesday? German?

Laverne. — er …

Tiffany. I think that's truly a brilliant idea. Brilliant! What a fantastic way to learn languages, isn't it? We could use a different one every day, couldn't we? Thursdays, Spanish. Fridays, Dutch ——

Laverne. Possibly, yes …

Tiffany. *(enthused)* I mean, we're generally dreadful in this country, aren't we? Never bother to learn anyone else's language, do we? And they're always learning ours.

During the next, **Tiffany** *removes her coat and goes off to the front door to hang it up.*

Laverne *takes the opportunity to smarten* **Winnie** *up a little.*

(off) I mean, you go to somewhere like Holland, they practically all speak English, don't they? Even little kids. Or Germany. Germany's the same. I mean, even, *even* let's face it, the French — they at least have a go. No, they all put us to shame.

Tiffany *returns, still talking.*

Golly. I really think you're on to a winner. Now all you have to do is to persuade everyone else to join in. *(to* **Winnie***) Bon! Bien! Excellente! Encore!* Bravo!

Winnie. Merci, mam'selle.

Tiffany. Oh, she's just enchanting. So sweet. How old did she say she was?

Laverne. *(proudly)* She's just coming up to nine. She'll be nine next month.

Tiffany. You must be so proud of her.

Laverne. *(modestly)* Yes, well … I don't tell her that, though!

Tiffany. I bet her daddy's proud of her, too. *(to* **Winnie***)* I bet you're your daddy's pride and joy, aren't you?

Winnie. Non, mam'selle.

Tiffany. No? Non?

Winnie. Mon père n'est pas ici. Il depart depuis quelques mois.

Laverne. Her dad's gone.

Tiffany. Oh, I am sorry. Was he very young?

Laverne. No, but she was. The one he went off with.

Tiffany. Oh. *(realizing)* Oh, I see. I'm so sorry, I thought you meant he was …

Laverne. He was old enough to know better.

Tiffany. *(Laverne's condition)* And now you're — ? Oh dear, how difficult for you. When's baby due?

Laverne. Another ten days.

Tiffany. Oh, dear. Shouldn't you be … ? I mean … ?

Laverne. I can manage. Soon as he's arrived, we're off, aren't we, girl? Soon as he's arrived …

Tiffany. Your husband?

Laverne. No, the baby! Not my husband, not him. We're best off without him, aren't we, Winnie?

Winnie *does not reply. A short silence.*

Tiffany. So you know it's a boy, then?

Laverne. Oh, yes.

Tiffany. How exciting! And have you settled on a name yet? That's always the tricky bit. Isn't it?

Laverne. Three. I've settled on three.

Tiffany. Oh, what are those?

Laverne. Jericho, Alexander, Samson …

Tiffany. Golly!

Winnie *rolls her eyes.*

What made you chose those? Jericho? That's terribly unusual. What made you choose Jericho?

Laverne. After my grand-dad. I've chosen three, that way he gets a choice. When he's little, he can either be Jerry or Alex or Sam. Then once he grows up if he wants to, he can choose one of the big ones …

Tiffany. How frightfully sensible. So he'll have masses of choices. I wish I'd been given choices when I was little.

All I got was Tiffany Louise. Which left me with Tiffy or Tiff or Lou. Which always makes me sound like a cross between a quarrel and lavatory. *(to* **Winnie***)* What about you? Did your mummy give you a choice of names as well?
Laverne. She's just the two, she has. Winona Marguerite.

Winnie *scowls.*

Tiffany. Marguerite? Wow! That's a great one! Marguerite!
Laverne. She's not too fond of that one, are you, Winnie? I've told her she might when she grows up. When she grows into it.
Tiffany. Yes, I know what you mean. You do need a bit of a cleavage, don't you, before you start calling yourself Marguerite? It's the sort of name that goes with breasts, isn't it?

Tiffany *laughs.* **Laverne** *smiles politely.* **Tiffany** *remembers there is a child present and checks herself. A slight pause.*

(*She slaps her face.*) Sorry. Where are your family from originally?
Laverne. They came from Martinique. My mother came over with my grandma nearly thirty years ago. We're planning to go back soon aren't we, Winnie?

Winnie *again does not reply.*

Tiffany. Ah! Hence the French! La belle Martinique. All is clear. How terrific! That's off the coast of Africa, isn't it?
Laverne. No, it's in the Caribbean.
Tiffany. Oh, yes, of course it is. *(slapping herself)* Come on, Tiffy!
Laverne. Fifteen point five miles south of Dominica and twenty-three miles north of St. Lucia.
Tiffany. Oh, yes. Got it! I think I was probably thinking of Mozambique.
Laverne. No, no, not Mozambique. Martinique.
Tiffany. Or possibly Madagascar? One of those. *(laughing)* God, aren't we hopeless in this country? We don't know where anything is, do we? Not just abroad, but anywhere. You know I don't think I could even find my way to Scunthorpe.
Laverne. I don't think I could.

The two smile at each other.

Tiffany. *(laughing)* Hopeless, aren't we? Absolutely hopeless. God, when I think of the fortune my parents splashed
out on my education. Honestly!
Laverne. Mine didn't.
Tiffany. Well, good for them. Save your money, I say! *(She
laughs.)*
Laverne. I still don't know nothing. *(She laughs.)*

Tiffany *laughs with her.*

   The **Man** *enters from the office.*

The **women** *look a bit guilty.*

Man. *(to* **Tiffany***)* Ah, you're here.
Tiffany. 'morning.
Man. How long you been out here?
Tiffany. Just a couple of minutes.
Laverne. Well, I must get on. Finish the kitchen. Excuse
me.
Man. Yes, you carry on, Mrs. — er ...
Tiffany. Sure you can manage?
Laverne. Oh, yes ...
Tiffany. I mean, don't for God's sake don't try lifting the
stove or anything, will you?
Laverne. I can manage.
Man. She can manage.
Laverne. Nice talking to you, Tiffany. See you later.

   Laverne *goes off to the kitchen.*

Tiffany. See you later, Laverne.
Man. *(softly, to* **Tiffany***)* What were you doing?
Tiffany. Just chatting.
Man. *(smiling, though meaning it)* I don't pay you to chat,
you know. Either of you.
Tiffany. Sorry, I thought you were on the phone.
Man. Come in here, then. We need to talk ... *(He starts
to move back towards the office.)* What did you call her just
then?
Tiffany. *(following him)* Who?
Man. Mrs. Whatsname? What did you call her?

Tiffany. Who, Laverne?

Man. Laverne? What sort of name's that?

Tiffany. It's her name.

Man. How do you find that out?

Tiffany. She just told me.

Man. She's worked here for ages, I've never known her name's Laverne. Laverne?

Tiffany. *(aware of* **Winnie***)* Shhh!

Man. Laverne? What sort of name's that for a cleaner?

Tiffany. *(to* **Winnie***)* You'll be all right there, will you darling?

Winnie. Oui merci, ma'mselle. Je suis très content.

Man. What's she talking in? French?

Tiffany. Yes.

Man. Why's she talking French?

Tiffany. She does on Tuesdays.

Man. Why the hell does she usually talk in French ——? *(His mobile rings. He checks it. Seeing the caller ID.)* Shit! It's her.

Tiffany. *(indicating the office, furtively)* You want to take it in there?

But the **Man** *has already answered.*

Man. Hallo, Paula … yes. … what? … who? … No, she's not here … of course she's not. … What makes you think she'd be here, for God's sake? … Bollocks … Paula, that is plain bollocks, darling … you are talking bollocks …

During the next, **Tiffany** *indicates that* **Winnie** *is in the room. The* **Man** *indicates that* **Tiffany** *should take* **Winnie** *into the office.*

Tiffany. *(under the phone call, softly, to* **Winnie***)* Come with me! This way! Come on, we can wait in here, Winnie …

Tiffany *bundles up* **Winnie***, helping her with her belongings, and steers her into the office.*

Man. *(as this happens, pacing)* … listen, Paula — Paula — Paula — where are you now? … No … no … because I was worried … I was, I was worried. … About you, who else? … Yes, I was … I was … Paula … Paula … Quieten down, love … will you just — QUIETEN DOWN, WOM-AN! *(kicking at the furniture, quieter)* Shit!!!

He moves towards the front door as his conversation starts to hot up. **Winnie** *is propelled by* **Tiffany** *into the office during the next.*

Yes! … *YES!* … Of course I was worried … well, why shouldn't I be, for God's sake? … You suddenly piss off in the middle of the bloody night, I've every reason to be fucking ——

The office door slams behind them, cutting off the **Man** *'s voice.*

The **Man** *exits.*

Simultaneously, the lights change abruptly to indicate the office area.

10.30 a.m.

Tiffany *tries to make everything appear normal for* **Winnie**.

Tiffany. He's just talking with someone … He gets quite excited sometimes but you musn't worry about it. He doesn't really mean it. Not really.

A further bellow of anger, off, from the hall. Pause.

(*Indicating the easy chair*) You want to sit there, darling.

Winnie *sits obediently, still holding her possessions.*

He's a very clever person. He's brilliant. He's actually quite famous. Did you know that? Have you ever seen him? On television. He has his own programme. Have you ever watched his programme? No? Surely you must have seen him? He was actually on the front cover of the *Radio Times*. No?

Winnie. (*shaking her head*) Non, mam'selle. Je ne vois pas le TV.

Tiffany. You don't watch television?

Winnie. (*shaking her head*) Non, mam'selle. Jamais.

Tiffany. What never? You never watch it? Well, you are a funny little girl, aren't you? I thought all children watched television. Does your mother not let you watch it?

Winnie. Oui. Mais je ne l'apprécie pas.
Tiffany. What? You don't like it? None of it?
Winnie. *(shrugging)* Non. Je le trouve être ennuyeux plutôt.
Tiffany. What do you like to do then?
Winnie. J'ai lu les livres. J'effectue mon travail d'école. J'ecris parfois.
Tiffany. Ecris? Oh, you write?
Winnie. Oui, mam'selle.
Tiffany. What? Poems?

Winnie *shakes her head.*

Tiffany. Stories?

Winnie *nods.*

Is that what you were doing just now? Writing?

Winnie *nods.*

(*reaching towards her*) May I see?

Winnie *clutches the exercise book to her more tightly.*

No? Is it secret? Your special secret? Is it about private things? Do you like to keep secrets, do you? I used to have secrets when I was a little girl. Things I would never, ever tell anyone. But the important thing to remember is, if you do write them down, to make sure no one never, ever sees them except you. It's good to have secrets when you're young. Maybe, as you grow up, they're not quite as magic … (*She tails off.*) Yep.

Pause.

When I was at school, you know, I used to keep a diary. Do you keep a diary? No?

Pause.

But I never let anyone see my diary. It was my most special, special secret book. And I used to keep it locked up. With a key. Until some boy went and …

Pause

I was at boarding school, you know. Do you know what a boarding school is? It's when you go away from your home, when your parents send you away — even though they tell you they still love you — they send you away to live with lots and lots of other children. But you're there all on your own.

Pause

And to start with you feel terribly, terribly sad being away from home but in the end you get used to it. And then you even start to like the school a little bit and some of the people there become your friends. And you may even start to love some of them, just a little. But it's a different sort of love, you see. It's what I call lonely love. There's all different sorts of love, you know. Did you know that?

Winnie *nods.*

But with lonely love, you see, it can never take the place of real love, however hard you try to make it. And the saddest thing of all is that in the end maybe because of it, you even start to love your parents a little tiny bit less. Do you see?

Pause.

So don't ever, ever let your mummy send you away. Because you love her very much, don't you?

Winnie *nods.*

And I can see she loves you very much, doesn't she?

Winnie *nods. From outside the door, another yell of anger from the Man*

Man. *(off, yelling)* OH, COME ON!!!!

Winnie *stares at the door.* **Tiffany** *searches round for something to distract the child. She snatches up the envelope she has brought.*

Tiffany. *(with the tone of a frenetic children's TV host)* Tell you what. I've got a great idea. While Mummy's busy, let's you and me watch this together, shall we?

She rips open the envelope and produces a DVD. It's a commercially mass-produced copy of a corporate video labelled, Fantacity!

This is something we've just finished. It's very exciting. Would you like to watch this with me? Would you?

Winnie *nods.*

Yes! Now, how do we work this thing. It's complicated. Everything he has is complicated, nothing's ever simple. Where does this go? Oh, yes. Then we can watch it on that big screen, can't we? (*slotting the disc into the console on the desk*) Be like going to the movies, won't it? You enjoy going to the movies, don't you?

Winnie. Non, mam'selle, je ne vais pas au cinema beaucoup.

Tiffany. Non? No? Never?

Winnie. Ma mère dit qu'il coûte trop d'argent.

Tiffany. *(half to herself)* Weird kid. Weird.

*She pulls out the desk chair to sit beside **Winnie**, grabbing the remote as she does so.*

There. That's a plasma screen. Have you ever seen one that big? The man who has everything, honestly! Every gadget under the sun, he's got it.

Tiffany *points the remote. After a second the (unseen) screen lights up and there's a burst of cheesy music. **Winnie** stares at the screen increasingly unimpressed. **Tiffany**, on the other hand, is in a state of considerable excitement.*

(*Over this introductory music*) I helped him on this, you know. Mainly typing the script and a little bit with the continuity. You know, if we're terribly lucky and watch very carefully, we might just catch a glimpse of me. Ever so briefly. If they haven't cut me out. (*Indicating the screen*) There! Just look at that! Isn't it fantastic?

*On the disc the music fades down slightly and the **Man**'s voice is heard.*

Man's voice.   Hi! It's my pleasure to introduce a new experience in the art of living. Welcome to the amazing world of Fantacity. I'm Kevin Tate and for the next few minutes, I'd like to show you around so you can see for yourselves some of the incredible features Fantacity has to offer you — yes, and that means you, Mr and Mrs Business Person.

Tiffany.   *(to* **Winnie***)* He's charismatic, isn't he? The camera adores him …

Man's voice.   So, hey, tell you what, why don't you and I stroll around a little so I can point out just a few of the extra special features Fantacity has to offer.

A short peak in the music.

(*in another acoustic*) Fantacity has been described as being part business park, part shopping mall. But, you know, neither of those descriptions can do Fantacity real justice. I prefer to describe it as a place where business and retail are free to meet and integrate with the consumer. It's a place where, at the end of the day, everyone goes home happy — and for those who prefer to stay on, well Fantacity stays open 24/7, catering for your every need.

Another brief music peak.

(*in another acoustic, again*) Fantacity offers workspace such as this for the business which thinks big — right down to the smaller scale — such as this — for smaller specialist firms and for those just starting up …

Another brief music peak. **Winnie**, *already bored, is beginning to slide down in her seat.* **Tiffany** *remains glued to the screen.*

(*in yet another acoustic*) And OK, retailers, in case you're feeling neglected, how about this for floor space? Imagine how your display would look in an environment like this. Or perhaps this? Or this?

The music peaks again.

Man's voice. All right, all right, I hear you saying, it's all very well but these are just offices and shops, I can see those anywhere, any time. What's so special about Fantacity? What on earth is someone like Kevin Tate getting so excited about? Well, I'll show you. Come with me to see the pleasure side of Fantacity.

Music peak.

(*in another acoustic*) Just take a look at this.

Tiffany. (*excitedly*) This is my bit, this my bit coming up! I'm a film star!

Man's voice. Here's what really caught my attention, what definitely got the five star, gold-plated Kevin Tate diamond seal of approval. This is one of the three magnificent swimming pools Fantacity has to offer. This is the largest of them, open free to all Fantacity users — shopper or salesperson, typist or tycoon …

Tiffany. That's me! That's me! That's me! There on the sun lounger!

Man's voice. … all absolutely free! (*with a little laugh in his voice*) Though that doesn't, I'm afraid, include the young lady!

Tiffany. God! That costume makes me look huge! So fat!

Man's voice. Moving along — if I can tear you away — moving along ——

The sound track stops abruptly. There's a brief blip and then Paula's voice interrupts.

Paula's voice. (*different acoustic, briskly*) Sorry to interrupt your tour of this ghastly little development, everyone. Hallo there, my name is Paula Hammond and I'm currently married to that deceitful little shit Kevin Tate …

Winnie *sits up again and takes notice.*

Tiffany. (*aghast*) Oh, my God. It's her!

Paula's voice. … yes, that's him, the forty-something year old, seen there drooling over Tiffany Cavendish, she's the tubby, super-annuated teenager on the sunbed.

During the next, **Tiffany** *grabs the remote and feverishly fumbles with the stop button.*

But what you might also be interested to learn, dear business people, is that those two are currently fucking each other's brains out — if that is even remotely possible — considering that neither of them has a solitary brain cell ——

Tiffany. *(finally freezing the disc)* Oh, my God! Oh, my God! Oh, my God!

She rushes out of the room forgetting **Winnie**.

(calling as she goes, in panic) Kevin! Kevin! KEVIN!

Winnie *sits for a moment, digesting what she has seen. She then takes up her note book and continues writing.*

Agitated voices outside.

11.30 a.m.

After a moment, **Tiffany** *returns with the* **Man** *following her.*

(Pointing at the screen, in panic) Look! It's her! She's on it! Look!

Man. *(staring at the screen)* What's she doing on there?

Tiffany. I told you, she's on our DVD.

Man. What DVD?

Tiffany. I keep telling you. The one we did for Fantacity.

Man. She can't be. *(grabbing the remote from her)* Give me that —

Tiffany. No! Don't play back any more of it!

Man. Why not? I want to see it … I want to see what that bitch has done!

Tiffany. Not in front of — *(indicating* **Winnie**, *mouthing)* — the kid!

Man. *(aware of* **Winnie**) Oh, yes. *(To* **Winnie**) You want to sit in the other room for a minute, kid? Just while we have a look at the DVD. We just discovered it may have …

Tiffany *helps* **Winnie** *up.*

Tiffany. … adult content.

Man. Wouldn't want you to see that. Your mum might not approve. Off you go! Chop! Chop!

Winnie. *(as she goes)* Oui, monsieur. Merci beaucoup.

Tiffany brings Winnie back to the hall/living-room area with all her gear. As she does so the lights crossfade briefly to the hall again.

The Man exits into the office during the next.

A clinking of plates from the kitchen.

Tiffany. *(registering this sound)* Listen, darling, perhaps you'd like to sit in the kitchen with Mummy? Keep her company. Would you like to do that? Jolly good.

Propelling Winnie through the kitchen doorway.

That's it, straight through here. Good girl.

Tiffany brings Winnie into the kitchen. The lights, again, follow them to the area. This is represented by a solid plain wood table and one or two chairs around it.

Laverne appears, looking weary and rather breathless.

Brought Winnie to see you, Mummy. She thought you might be lonely.

Laverne. I hope she's not been getting in people's way.

Tiffany. No, no, no. Not at all. We've been having a lovely chat, haven't we, Winnie?

Laverne. Have you been getting under their feet, Winnie?

Winnie. Non, Maman. J'ai été tranquille comme souris.

Tiffany. She's been as good as gold.

Man. *(off, angrily)* Tiffy! Tiffy!

Tiffany. Excuse me, must get back. Masses to do.

Tiffany hurries out.

Laverne. Sit there then. Don't get under my feet either. I've nearly finished in here.

Winnie sits at the table and lays out her stuff once more.

It was like a hurricane had been through this kitchen. God knows what they were up to last night, those two. Hurling food at each other, that's what it looked like. I'm going to give this a final wipe, then I'm off upstairs to do the bedrooms.

Laverne *moves out of view to clean something.*

Winnie. You all right, Mum?
Laverne. *(off)* I'm all right. Why shouldn't I be?
Winnie. You look tired.
Laverne . *(off)* I'll have a sit down in a minute.
Winnie. You better had.
Laverne. *(off)* Have you been practising your French?
Winnie. Yeah.
Laverne. *(off)* Pardon? Qu'avez vous dit?
Winnie. *(wearily)* Oui, Maman.
Laverne. *(off)* That's better! C'est bien!

Winnie *sighs.*

Laverne *reappears with a half-finished mug of tea and an opened can of Coke which she plonks in front of Winnie.*

Laverne. Voilà!
Winnie. *(automatically)* Merci, Maman.

A silence between them. From off, an angry yell from the **Man**, *a crash, and a cry from* **Tiffany**.

Laverne. What they up to now then, for heavens sake? *(She sits at the table to finish her tea.)* You see? What do I always say to you? What did that man tell us in church the other day? All this money and they're still not happy. Let that be a warning to you, Winnie. It can't bring you happiness, darling. Be warned, darling.

Winnie *is silent, drinking her Coke.*

When your grandad and grandma, when they first got here, when they first arrived in this country, my mum told me they were the happiest two people in the whole world. And you know why she said that was? They were like Adam and Eve, she said, who had nothing in the world, no possessions, no money, nothing. Who'd just walked out of Paradise. And from then on, he found work, she found work, they made a bit of money, bought a little house, filled it with things, worldly possessions and everything went downhill from there. The more they had, the more miserable they became. Well, we'll soon be walking back to Paradise, darling, you, me and little Jericho. Any day now. I've nearly saved enough. Then the three of us — off we'll go — on that plane. You'll see.

Winnie. *(softly)* Not if you die, we won't.

Laverne. *(startled)* What?

Winnie. Not if you die.

Laverne. What are you talking about? Die? I'm not going to die, you stupid thing.

Winnie. You might do.

Laverne hugs Winnie to her.

Laverne. Who said anything about dying? Don't worry, I'm not dying, not yet. No way.

Winnie. You might if you don't take care of yourself, you might.

Laverne. Be a few years yet, I can promise.

> **Tiffany** *bursts into the room, distraught. She has apparently forgotten that* **Winnie** *and* **Laverne** *are in there. She slaps her face a couple of times, in an attempt to control herself. Looking round the room, she runs out of view briefly and returns with a length of hastily torn-off kitchen roll. She runs out again, attempting to mop her eyes and blow her nose simultaneously.*

The **Man** *is heard calling her.*

Man. *(off, conciliatory)* Tiffy … Tiff! Come on, now! Don't be silly!

Laverne. *(significantly gesturing after* **Tiffany***)* There! You see. Be warned. *(finally draining her mug and rising)* Well, I can't sit around here, can I? *(indicating* **Winnie***'s can of Coke)* Finished with that?

Winnie *swigs the last mouthful. The doorbell rings.*

Oh. Somebody else arriving. I hope someone's going to answer it.

Laverne *promptly scoops up the empty can. She momentarily disappears from view, getting rid of the empties.*

(*off*) How are you getting on with your homework, then? Finished your essay yet?
Winnie. Not quite.
Laverne. (*off*) "My Wonderful Day." How's it getting on?
Winnie. It isn't finished.
Laverne. (*off*) You'll have Mrs Crackle after you if you don't finish your essay.
Winnie. Not the essay, the day. The day isn't finished yet, is it?
Laverne. (*off, not hearing her*) You'll be in all sorts of trouble, you don't hand it in first thing tomorrow morning.
Winnie. I will. (*muttering*) Soon as today's finished, I will.

Laverne *re-emerges with the vacuum cleaner.*

Laverne. Right, you sit here quietly. Don't move. Don't get in nobody's way. I'll be back in a minute, then I'll take you home, all right?
Winnie. OK.
Laverne. Tell you what, you can read me it tonight, your essay. How about that?
Winnie. Probably.
Laverne. (*as she makes to leave*) And keep practising your French, too. Promise is a promise.
Winnie. (*wearily*) Oui, maman. (*She pulls a face behind her mother's back.*)

12.30 p.m.

As **Laverne** *leaves, she nearly collides in the doorway with the* **Man** *and his newly arrived visitor,* **Josh**, *about the same age as the* **Man**. **Laverne** *steps back to allow them to pass.*

Josh. Whoops! Mothers and children first.
Man. (*waving* **Laverne** *through*) All right, Mrs. ... er ... you come through first, come through ...

Laverne. Thank you, Mr Tate. *(to* **Josh***)* Good morning. Finished in here. All clear now.

Josh. *(a bit the worse for wear)* 'morning.

Laverne *goes out with the vacuum.*

Man. Sorry to drag you out, mate.

Josh. No, as I say, it was Colin's leaving do last night and one thing led to another, as you'll well know ... *(seeing* **Winnie***)* Hallo, hallo, who's this then? Where did this little thing spring from? Who are you, then?

Man. Her kid. The cleaner's kid.

Josh. Hallo. You're pretty, aren't you? Like your mummy. Your mummy's pretty, too. Hallo. Want to say hallo, do you?

Winnie. Bonjour, monsieur.

Josh. Eh?

Man. She doesn't speak English.

Josh. Really?

Man. She only speaks French.

Josh. Does she?

Man. Apparently.

Josh. Her mum speaks English.

Man. Oh, yes, she does.

Josh. How come she has a kid who only speaks French?

Man. *(slightly impatiently)* I don't know, do I?

Josh. She must speak English if her mum does.

Man. I've never heard her speak English, anyway.

Josh. Do you speak English? Parlez-vous Anglais?

Winnie. Non, monsieur. Je ne parle pas l'anglais, pas aujourd'huis. Je parle seulment français le mardi.

Josh. What did she say?

Man. There you are, what did I tell you?

Josh. I never heard of that before. A mum who speaks English and a kid who ——

Man. So, anyway. What did you find out, then?

Josh. Do you mind if I get that glass of water ...?

Man. Yes, go ahead, help yourself.

Josh *disappears from view momentarily.*

Josh. *(off)* I'm that dehydrated after last night ... No, as I was saying, as soon as I got to your office, the minute you called me — which of these buttons do you press to get water —— ?

Man. Either one. Green one's for ambient. Blue one's ice cold.

Josh. *(off)* Oh, yes — there you go — what's wrong with good old fashioned taps? — yes, I say — I fast forwarded through the first two or three DVD's in the batch, just to check whether they were corrupted as well — and …

Man. What, all of them?

Josh returns with a glass of water.

Josh. *(as he comes back)* As far as I could tell, every single one. Good job you didn't send them out, wasn't it?

Man. *(pounding the table)* Shit! Shit! Shit!

Josh. *(admonishingly)* Kev!

Man. What?

Josh. *(indicating **Winnie**)* Better watch the language.

Man. What bloody language? She doesn't even speak it. No, truth be told, I should have chucked Paula out of the bedroom window last night when I had the chance.

Josh. *(sitting)* Bad?

Man. Terrible.

Josh. Where's she now?

Man. I don't know. Walked out. Finally.

Josh. When?

Man. Last night, early this morning. I was asleep. Woke up, she'd taken off …

Josh. Well …

Man. Finally. At long last. And I pray for ever. *(reflecting)* You know, I think she must be slightly mad.

Josh. Paula?

Man. Genetic, you know. Faulty genes. Violent streak. There's a streak of violence in her which is unnatural. I mean, in a woman it's not natural is it? I mean a woman's natural nature is not a violent one, is it?

Josh. I've known violent women. Very violent ones.

Man. No, but they were unnatural. That's my point. I mean, with men violence is a natural ingredient, it's germane in their nature. But women. I mean, take the phrase "feminine qualities" — what are they? — gentle, quiet spoken — submissive — agreeable — soft — don't argue with you …

Josh. *(doubtfully)* Yes … I don't think I've met many of those. Maybe I've been unlucky. I mean, they may start out that way — but then they — you know — go off …

Man. Paula went off. Like last week's milk. She always agreed with me to start with. Always. Even when I had to talk her round first. No, she's mad. Certifiable. I wed a lunatic, Josh.

Josh. So. That's it then?

Man. Marry an angel, divorce a monster. That's what my dad used to say. He should have known. Got through four of them, didn't he, before we buried him.

Josh. Well. I have to say it's been a long time coming.

They reflect gloomily.

I was your best man.

Man. Yes.

Josh. She looked lovely, then. She did, she looked like an angel. Beautiful. I really fancied Paula then. Not that she'd have … with me. Only had eyes for you in those days.

Man. Did you try it then? With her? With my wife? What, on our bloody wedding day? You're joking!

Josh. Well … I may have hinted to her. In a roundabout way. You know, jokingly, like. You know, if you ever get bored of him …

Man. What did she say to that?

Josh. She told me to — *(with a brief glance at* **Winnie***)* — you know — get stuffed.

Man. Quite right, you cheeky berk! *(slight pause)* You're welcome to her now, mate.

They laugh. A silence. **Winnie** *watches them covertly.* **Josh** *notices this.* **Winnie** *resumes her writing again.*

Josh. *(regarding her suspiciously)* You sure that kid doesn't speak English?

Man. Why?

Josh. I get the feeling she does.

Man. No. She doesn't. Unless she's lying.

Josh. Lying? Why should she be lying?

Man. I don't know. She's a woman, isn't she? They're all bloody liars.

Pause.

I'm going to have a beer. Want some more of that?

Josh. God, come on, be fair. Two glasses of water in one day? I'm already over my limit.

The **Man** *goes off momentarily.*

Man. *(off)* Tiffy went crazy as well.
Josh. Tiffany?
Man. *(off)* She was the one that saw it first. Ran upstairs. Howling her eyes out.
Josh. Why she do that? What made her react like that?

The **Man** *returns with a can of beer.*

Man. *(coming back)* Search me. Paula calling her fat, probably.
Josh. Fat?
Man. She calls her that on the DVD.
Josh. What? Fat? Tiffy's not fat, is she?
Man. *(sitting)* Try telling her. Anyway she's upstairs now, lying on the bed. Texting. Stupid kid. *(sinking his head in his hands)* Gawd! What a mess!

Josh *becomes aware of* **Winnie** *again.*

Josh. What's she writing there?
Man. What?
Josh. What's that kid writing? What's that you're writing, kid?
Winnie. Pardon, monsieur?
Josh. *(reaching out for her book)* Here. Show me.

He grabs the book and he and **Winnie** *tussle with it momentarily.*

Man. Look, Josh, leave her, for God's sake. We'll have the mother suing us for molestation next, won't we? That's all I need.

Josh *draws back.*

Josh. *(to* **Winnie***)* Sorry. Pardonnez-moi.

Pause. The Man takes a swig of beer.

Man. So. You reckon Paula may have corrupted the whole batch?

Josh. So far as I could tell.

Man. How could she do that? How the hell could she have managed that?

Josh. She's a resourceful woman, isn't she?

Man. *(bitterly)* Oh, yes.

Josh. Film director, isn't she? Knows about these things. Didn't she used to edit?

Man. Oh, yes.

Josh. There you go then. Piece of cake for her. Won that BAFTA, didn't she?

Man. Don't remind me. She keeps it by the bed. Every time I wake up, I'm reminded of it, staring at me …

Josh. Probably she's proud of it.

Man. Probably to piss me off.

Josh. Yes, well, whatever. She most probably got at the original tape. It was shot on video originally, wasn't it? And then copied to DVD.

Man. Well, didn't anybody notice while they were copying it, for God's sake?

Josh. Why should they?

Man. Calling me a deceitful little shit and all that? Somebody must have noticed, surely?

Josh. They run these things off by the hundreds, Kev. High speed copying. Takes a matter of seconds, that's all.

Man. *(rising)* Well. They'll all have to be withdrawn, won't they? Cost us thousands. Not to mention the good will. Well, she's won. She's got what she wanted, hasn't she? She's shafted us.

Josh. At least she didn't cut up your shirts.

Man. *(laughing)* I should be so lucky.

Josh. My wife did. Before she kicked me out.

Man. I'm going to look in on Tiffy, see how she is. See you in a minute.

Josh. Right.

Man. Tell you what, it's nearly one o'clock. We'll all nip round the corner for some lunch, if Tiff's up to it. Fancy a bit of lunch?

Josh. I'm up for that. I'm ravenous. We had this huge Indian meal at Colin's leaving do, I woke up this morning I was starving. Mind you, I did lose most of it during the night.

Man. Yes, well. See you in a minute.

*The **Man** goes out, swilling the last of his beer.*

Josh *and* **Winnie** *sit together silently for a second.* **Winnie** *crouching over her exercise book, writing.* **Josh** *sips water. In a moment, he gets restless.*

1 p.m.

Josh. Hey — hey, kid. What's your name, then? Eh? What's your name? *(in quite appalling French)* Quel nomme? Vous?
Winnie. Je m'appelle Winnie, m'sieur.
Josh. Winnie. That's nice. Winnie the Pooh, eh? *(He laughs.)* That what they call you at school, then, is it? Winnie the Pooh?
Winnie. Non, m'sieur.
Josh. No? Hey, Winnie, do you want to see a magic trick, then? I'll show you a magic trick, shall I? You don't have to speak English for this. I'll show you. I bet you can't guess how I do this? Bet you can't guess. Now then, first thing is, do I have a coin? *(fumbling in his pocket and producing a coin)* Yes, yes, I do. I've got one here. Now watch very carefully. Regardez, s'ivvous play.

Winnie *watches him politely.*

(Making magical gestures with the coin) Now, watch … *regardez* carefully … are you watching? *(He does a piece of sleight of hand — possibly a "french drop"— to make the coin apparently disappear)* Voilà! Say disapparay! *Oui!*

Winnie *nods solemnly. She does not seem that impressed.*

Say magic, eh? Where's it gone, then? Where's it gone? Shall I make it come back? Come back again? Yes? Retourneray? *Oui?*

More gestures.

And … *un, deux, trois … et … voilà!* *(producing it from behind her ear)* How did it get there? Magic! How did it get there, then? Eh? Eh?

Josh *laughs, shakes his head.* **Winnie** *is silent. She smiles faintly and politely, the way children do when humouring an adult.*

My little girl used to love that. How did you do that, Dad? How did you do that? Do it again? Do it again? That's what she used to say.

Pause.

I think she was probably a little bit younger than you, Winnie, when I used to do it for her. My little girl. Her name's Amber. You like that name? Amber. Unusual. Her mum chose that. Amber.

Pause.

Little Amber. I think the world of her. She adores me. I go round to visit her every other weekend, regular like clockwork. She's always waiting there for me. Just inside the front gate. Looking out for me. Eager little face. Waiting. Little matching hat and coat. Waiting for me to take her out somewhere special. Give her a treat. A boat ride on the river. Or the zoo. Amber loves the zoo. Especially the gibbons. You know, the little tiny monkeys. They make her laugh and laugh. Yes, gibbons …

Pause. He smiles. **Winnie** *watches him.*

Yes, she means the world to me. Little Amber. She adores me. Worships the ground I walk on. Whenever I bring her home again to her mum, you know, after we've both been out together for the day, she never wants to come home again. She kicks and screams. Clinging on to the gate. Her mum has to drag her inside. Terrible.

Pause.

Enough to break your heart, really.

Pause.

All the same, they're great days. Wouldn't miss them. Either of us.

Pause.

(*suddenly tearful*) God, I miss her some days that much. I don't mind saying.

From the hall, the vacuum starts up.

(*wiping his eyes*) Yes, well. Not that you'd understand any of that, would you, kid? Even if you could talk the language. (*He rises suddenly rather depressed. Moving to the door.*) You'll have to wait till you grow up for that, won't you?

Josh *goes out.*

Winnie *sits alone for a moment. Then resumes her writing with fresh zeal. The vacuuming continues for a second or two. Then there is a cry from* **Laverne**.

(*off*) You all right there, my love?
Laverne. (*off*) Yes, thank you. It was just a — I'll be fine.
Josh. (*off*) You sure?
Laverne. (*off*) Yes, it was just a — little — I get them from time to — (*as she has another one*) Wooh!

Winnie *rises and tentatively moves to the doorway.*

Josh. (*off*) Just a second I'll get some help, my love. I think you may need a bit of help …
Laverne. (*off*) No, please don't bother people. It's really nothing ——
Josh. (*off, calling*) Somebody! Can we have some help here, please? (*to* **Winnie**) You wait in there, darling!
Laverne. (*off*) Stay in there, Winnie. I'm all right, darling, Mummy's all right!

Winnie *obediently lingers reluctantly in the doorway. The kitchen remains lit.*

Tiffany. (*off, approaching*) What's happened? What's going on?
Man. (*off, simultaneously*) Somebody calling?

In the following section, the voices overlap as they cope with the emergency. Throughout this **Laverne** *alternates between reassuring people she's fine and sudden little cries as she experiences early labour pains. Sometime during this, the vacuum gets switched off.*

Laverne. *(off)* … I'm fine, I'm fine, please don't bother to … Ah! … I need probably to get to the … Wooh! *(another spasm)* … hospital … etc.

Josh. *(off, over this)* Sit down, now. You sit down here.

Tiffany. *(off, simultaneously)* What's happening? Is she all right?

Josh. *(off)* I think she might be going into labour …

Tiffany. *(off)* She certainly is …

Man. *(off)* I'll phone the ambulance. Hang on, I'll phone the ambulance …

Winnie. *(in the doorway, apprehensively)* Mum … Mum!

Laverne. *(off)* You're to wait in there, Winnie! I'm all right! I'm OK. *(another cry)* AH!

Josh. *(off, suddenly alarmed)* Oh, my God! Tiffy! Tiffy? What's happening here?

Tiffany. *(off)* Oh, no ——

Josh. *(off)* Is she having it?

Tiffany. *(off)* Wait there! Wait there!

Josh. *(off)* What's happening?

Tiffany. *(off)* It's just her waters … her waters … wait!

Josh. *(off)* Jesus! Look at that!

Laverne. *(off)* Oh, I'm sorry, I'm terribly sorry … it's your sofa, your lovely sofa …

Tiffany *comes rushing into the kitchen, nearly knocking* **Winnie** *over.*

Tiffany. *(as she rushes in, slightly panicked)* Whoops! Sorry, love! Out the way! Out the way!

Winnie. Mum?

Laverne. *(off, calling after* **Tiffany***)* Tell Winnie she's to wait in there!

Tiffany.. It's all right, love, nothing to worry about … wait here …

Josh. *(off, calling)* Oh, God. Tiffy!

Tiffany. *(as she goes)* …it's all perfectly natural …

Laverne. *(off)* Aaah!

Tiffany *disappears from view within the kitchen and returns swiftly with an assorted armload of hand towels, tea towels and paper towels, anything she can find that's remotely absorbent.*

Winnie. *(calling through the door, again)* Mum? Mum?

Laverne. *(off)* You wait in there, Winnie, do you hear me, you're to wait in there! Don't worry, I'm all right! Aah!!

Tiffany. *(as she returns)* You're to wait in here, darling. Your mother's just — she's just been taken a little bit … unawares …

Josh. *(off, yelling)* TIFFY! Quickly!

Tiffany *rushes out again.*

Tiffany. *(as she goes)* She's going into labour, that's all! Stay there! It's perfectly natural! It happens to everyone!

Man. *(off)* She wanted to know if it was a genuine emergency. Stupid cow. Of course it's a bloody emergency.

Laverne. *(off)* I'm terribly sorry. I'll clean it up later, don't worry!

Tiffany. *(off, to* **Laverne***)* For God's sake sit still, woman!

Josh. *(off)* You sit still now, Mrs — er … You sit still.

Winnie *reluctantly loiters in the kitchen. The sounds from the other room continue but more quietly now as things calm down a bit.* **Winnie** *sits down at the table while she waits. She is too distracted to return to her writing. She fidgets in her seat, waiting, rocking to and fro.*

1.45 p.m.

Laverne, *with* **Tiffany,** *appears in the doorway.* **Josh,** *in attendance, hovers behind, seemingly ready to catch* **Laverne** *if she falls.*

Winnie *rises.* **Laverne** *is obviously very shaky but doing her best to hide things from* **Winnie.**

Winnie. *(anxiously)* Mum?

Laverne. *(uncertainly)* Now, I'm all right, darling. You're not to worry. Mum's just off to have her baby. And then as soon as she has, you can come and visit at the hospital.

Now, if I need to stay in overnight — they may want me to stop in — I'm arranging for you to sleep over at Mrs Copthorne's, all right? With her Sophie. You get on well with Sophie, don't you?

Winnie nods.

Now, Mr. Tate's very kindly said that for the rest of this afternoon just until Mrs. Copthorne gets home from work, Mr. Tate says you can stop here with them. Isn't that kind of him? Ooo! (*She gets another contraction.*) Another one! They're getting quicker! Now, you're to be big and grown up while I'm gone, do you hear? Don't you get under people's feet. Finish your essay. Practise your French. Promise, me? Promise your mum?

Winnie *nods.*

Tiffany. We'll look after her, Mummy, don't worry.
Laverne. Soon as it arrives, I'm going in the ambulance. You be a good girl. I'll see you very soon, darling.

Winnie *runs and clings to her mother.*

Winnie. (*softly*) You take care of yourself, Mum.
Josh. (*to* **Tiffany**) I knew it! The kid speaks English!
Tiffany. (*to* **Josh**) Of course she does!
Josh. (*vindicated*) I said she did! I said!
Winnie. (*still clinging*) Mum?

The doorbell rings.

Laverne. I'll be fine. Don't worry. (*another contraction*) Woo! That's your little brother. Can you feel him? Little Jericho jumping about in there?
Man. (*off*) It's here! Ambulance is here!

Winnie *continues to cling on to her mother.*

Josh. (*mystified, to* **Tiffany** *softly*) Jericho?
Tiffany. (*to* **Josh**) Sssh! (*softly, to* **Laverne**) It's here.

Laverne *gently prises* **Winnie** *from her.*

Laverne *(kissing her gently)* Bye-bye, darling. See you soon.
Au 'voir.
Winnie Au 'voir, Maman. Soin de prise.

   Laverne *goes out,* **Tiffany** *and* **Josh** *following her.*

Winnie, *on her own again, mooches round the kitchen. Despite
her mother's reassurances, she remains a little anxious. From the
living-room, there is the sound of further voices, farewells and the
front door closing. Further muffled voices. A pause.*

   Then the **Man**, **Tiffany** *and* **Josh** *all enter together.*

They stare at her. **Winnie** *stares at them. They appear to be something of a deputation.*

2.15 p.m.

Man. *(rather formally)* Right. Winnie … that is your name,
isn't it? Winnie?

Winnie *nods. The* **Man** *is clearly not comfortable talking to a
child for any length of time.*

   Now, Winnie. I understand you speak English perfectly
well, so … Now, while your mum's gone, we're all here
to look after you. So — I've got some work to do. And
— once she's tidied up in there, Tiffany's going to be
helping me with that in the office. In the meantime —
Josh — Uncle Josh will sit with you in the kitchen here.
So — anything you want … you've only got to ask him
for it. Preferably in English. So, anything you want right
now, kid?

Winnie *shakes her head.*

Tiffany. *(softly)* She might want something to eat, Kev.
Man. You want something to eat, do you?

Winnie *shakes her head.*

   No?

Tiffany. It's after two o'clock. She hasn't had her lunch, has she?

Josh. I haven't had lunch yet, either.

Man. Nor have I.

Tiffany. Wouldn't you like a little bite of lunch, darling?

Winnie *shakes her head.*

   No? You sure?

Winnie *shakes her head.*

Man. No. She doesn't want lunch.

Tiffany. She probably hasn't had anything since her breakfast. She might like a little bite.

Man. She doesn't want any.

Tiffany. She's probably starving. I am.

Josh. I'm ravenous. I'd like some lunch.

Man. I wouldn't mind a spot of lunch, either. Tell you what, we'll all of us go out and have lunch! How about that?

Tiffany. Lovely!

Josh. Great!

Tiffany. *(to* **Winnie***)* You'd like that, Winnie, wouldn't you? Come out and have lunch with us all?

Winnie *shakes her head.*

   No? (*to the* **Man**) She doesn't want to go out.

Man. No?

Tiffany. No.

Man. Why not?

Tiffany. I don't know. She just doesn't.

Man. *(irritated)* Why the hell doesn't she want lunch?

Josh. Maybe she's not hungry.

Man. Well, she can just sit there, then. She doesn't have to eat, does she? If she doesn't want to? She can just sit there, can't she, watch us while we three eat.

Josh *(to* **Winnie***)* Would you like to do that, then? Come out and watch us eat? You'd enjoy that, wouldn't you?

Winnie *shakes her head again.*

Man. I'll pay. *(to* **Winnie***)* Don't worry I'm paying.

Winnie *shakes her head again.*

(*frustrated*) Jesus! Well, we'll just have to leave her here, won't we? (*to* **Winnie**) Stay behind here, sit on your own then.

Tiffany. We can't do that!

Josh. We couldn't do that, Kev!

Man. Why not? She doesn't want to come with us! She can stay here!

Tiffany. We can't go off and have lunch and leave the kid on her own?

Man. Why not?

Tiffany. She's nine years old!

Man. Well, what are we going to do, then?

Josh. We can't go out without the kid, Kev.

Man. She'll be all right. Writing her bloody novel, isn't she?

Tiffany. We cannot leave a nine-year old child alone in this house, I'm sorry.

Josh. No, that wouldn't be right, Kev. She might start playing with matches or something.

Man. Matches?

Josh. You know. Sharp objects. Razor blades.

Man. Great. Not only are we now glorified babysitters, we're also looking after a bloody juvenile suicide risk, are we? (*He glares frustratedly at* **Winnie**.) Well, I tell you this, I for one am not going to starve because of her. I am going round the corner for some lunch. Anyone wants to come with me, I'll see you there. If not then bugger you! (*angrily to* **Winnie**) That includes you, Emily Brontë!

Tiffany. For God's sake, Kev … Don't yell at her like that. She's a kid.

Man. Well. She drives me bloody nuts. First she's French, then she's English. First she wants lunch, then she doesn't want bloody lunch. I hate kids, I loathe them. I'll be in the office.

The **Man** *goes out.*

Tiffany. (*calling after him*) I thought you said you were going out?

Man. (*off, angrily*) I'm not eating on my own, am I?

A silence.

Tiffany. *(after a pause)* I'll tell you what, why don't I rustle together something for us here? For those that want it.
Josh. That'd be nice. I'm starving.

   Tiffany *moves out of view momentarily.*

Tiffany. *(as she goes)* If I can find something … *(Off)* There ought to be something here to nibble on …

A slight pause.

   Then **Tiffany** *re-appears.*

   (returning) No. There's absolutely nothing in the fridge, it's completely empty.
Josh. Yes, that sounds like Paula. Never the great provider, was she?
Tiffany. I'll go out and try and buy us all a sandwich, shall I?
Josh. That'd be nice.
Tiffany. There should be somewhere round here, even in this area … I'll see if he wants one. *(to* **Winnie***)* Would you like me to bring you back a sandwich, darling?

Winnie *shakes her head.*

Josh. No. She doesn't want a sandwich.
Tiffany. *(as she goes out, concerned)* She ought to eat something …

   Tiffany leaves.

2.45 p.m.

Winnie *sits down again.* **Josh** *wanders round the kitchen, aimlessly.*

Josh. Well, I'm starving. I don't know about you, kid.

He disappears momentarily.

(*Off*) No, she's quite right. Nothing. Couple of cans of beer and a clove of garlic. The cupboard is bare.

Winnie *gropes in her schoolbag and produces a chocolate bar which she opens and starts to eat.*

Josh *returns and stares at her.*

He sits and watches **Winnie** *as she eats.*

Nice? Is that nice, then? It looks nice.

Winnie *nods.*

My daughter, Amber, she adores those. I've seen her eat, what, four or five of those, straight after the other. Why she isn't the size of a house, I do not know.

Winnie *munches on.*

(*eyeing the remains of her bar, longingly*) Mind you, can't blame her. Bit more-ish, those. Know what I mean? They're a bit more-ish. One is never enough, is it? I bet you can't eat just the one. I bet you can't. I bet you've got another one hidden away somewhere. I bet you have, haven't you?

Winnie *nods.*

Yes! I knew it. Got another one, haven't you? Sneaky!

Winnie *nods.*

Yes. Tell you what. Want to share your other one, do you? With me? Want to share it, eh?

Winnie *shakes her head.*

No? Come on. That's a bit mean, isn't it? Bit selfish. Ah! I know! I bet your mum told you not to share sweets with strangers, is that it?

Winnie *nods.*

Right. She's quite right. Fair enough. That's what I always say to Amber. Never trust strangers. They may look friendly …

Winnie *finishes the bar and, scrumpling up the paper, looks for somewhere to put it.*

(*indicating*) There. The bin's just under there, do you see it?

Winnie *moves to the unseen bin and disappears from view momentarily.*

Josh *hesitates, trying to avoid temptation. He licks his lips and then, swooping on Winnie's schoolbag, starts to rifle through it searching for the other chocolate bar.*

Winnie *returns and catches him at it.*

Josh *stops guiltily, his hand half inside the school bag.* **Winnie** *stares at him blankly.* **Josh** *withdraws his hand to find he is holding a book which has a bookmark sticking out.*

(*covering his tracks*) Just having a look to see what you're reading. What's this, then? (*Inspecting the cover*) *The Secret Garden.* Oh, yes, that sounds exciting. This what you're reading then? It's a good thick book, isn't it? (*He examines it and then opens the book at its marked place*) You read this far, then? Well, I'm impressed. I'm very impressed. Small print, too. Not a lot of pictures. I think this might be a bit beyond Amber, even though she's older. The longest book she's ever read is the leaflet for her mobile phone. You enjoy reading then, do you? That's a good thing. Stand you in very good stead when you're older. Reading. Broadens your mind. Ruins your eyesight but broadens your mind. I regret never reading. I never read as a kid. My dad used to say to me, for God's sake, son, stop leaping about, sit down and read a good book. But I never did, never took heed of him. Now look at me, perfect twenty-twenty vision and ignorant as buggery. (*slight pause*) Sorry.

Pause.

Tell you what. While we're waiting, why don't you read me a bit? Could you do that? Out loud? In English? Would you like to do that?

Winnie *nods an if-I-must sort of nod. We get the impression that she'll agree to anything just to shut* **Josh** *up.*

(*returning the book to her*) Here you are. Hang on! Hang on! Just get comfy.

He settles in the easy chair. **Winnie** *continues to sit at the table.*

There we go. That's better. Right, away you go, kid. Broaden my mind.
Winnie. Je commence a partir du commencement?
Josh. What's that? No, I said, you can read it in English
Winnie. Do you want me to go from the beginning?
Josh. No, no. Just from where you got up to, darling. I'll soon pick it up. Don't worry. I'm like lightning, me.

Winnie *starts to read slowly and carefully at first. Then, as the narrative takes hold, with slightly more speed and gusto.* **Josh** *sits back listening with his eyes closed. Soon he falls asleep*

Winnie. (*reading*) "Chapter Four. Martha. When she opened her eyes in the morning it was because a young house-maid had come into her room to light the fire" ——
Josh. Ah! Those were the days, eh?
Winnie. (*reading*) — "to light the fire" ——
Josh. Gone are the days of waking up to young house-maids, eh?
Winnie. (*reading*) — "and was kneeling on the hearth" ——
Josh. — it's all alarm clocks and Radio Two these days, isn't it —— ?
Winnie. (*fairly politely*) M'avez-vous laissé lire ceci, s'il vous plaît?
Josh. Yes, yes, sorry. Carry on, kid.
Winnie. (*reading*) — "and was kneeling on the hearth-rug raking out the cinders noisily."
Josh No central heating in those days …

Winnie *(shooting him a look, then continuing)* "Mary lay and
watched her for a few moments and then began to look
about the room. She had never seen a room at all like it,
and thought it curious and gloomy. The walls were covered with … *(an unfamiliar word)* — tape-stry with a forest
scene … *(another one)* — em-embro-idered — embroi-
dered on it. There were fanatic-ally — fanatically dressed
people under the trees and in the distance there was a
glimpse of the turrets of a castle. There were hunters and
horses and dogs and ladies. Mary felt as if she were in the
forest with them. Out of a deep window she could see a
great climbing stretch which seemed to have no trees on
it. And to look rather like an endless dull puplish — pur-
plish — sea.
'What is that?' she said, pointing out of the window.
Martha, the young housemaid, who had just risen to her
feet, looked, and pointed also.
'That there?' she said.
'Yes.'
'That's th' moor,' with a good natured grin. 'Does tha'
like it?'
'No,' answered Mary. 'I hate it.'
'That's because th'art not used to it,' Martha said, going
back to her hearth. 'Tha' thinks it's too big an' bare now.
But tha' will like it.'
'Do you?' inquired Mary."

Josh *is asleep. Under the next, he starts to snore softly.*

Tiffany *creeps in. She has a wrapped sandwich in a bag.*

(continuing, unaware of this) "'Aye, that I do,' answered
Martha, cheerfully polishing away at the grate. 'I just love
it. It's none bare. It's covered wi' growing things as smells
sweet. It's fair lovely in spring an' summer when th' gorse
an' broom an' heather's in flower. It smells o' honey an'
there's such a lot o' fresh air — an' th' sky looks so high
an' th' bees and skylarks makes such a noise hummin'
an' singin'. Eh! I wouldn't live away from th' moor for
anythin'"—— *(She breaks off.)*

They notice that **Josh** *is asleep, snoring slightly more loudly now.*
Tiffany *slides the wrapped sandwich bag on to the table and*

indicates that it is intended for **Josh**. **Tiffany**, *anxious not to wake him, puts her finger to her lips and mouths to* **Winnie**, *pointing to the office to indicate that that's where the* **Man** *and she will be if they're needed.* **Winni**e *nods*

Tiffany *creeps out again*

As **Winnie** *continues to read, Josh's snoring increases in volume*

(*continuing, also with increased volume*) "Mary listened to her with a grave and puzzled exp-expression. The native servants she had been used to in India were not in the least like this. They were obs-obsqy-obs ... and serv-servil"
———

She tuts and gives up. The combination of difficult words and the competition from **Josh**, *are too much for her. She reads on silently for a bit, her lips moving slightly. She gets absorbed in the book. As she reads, she absently reaches out for the sandwich and, sliding it out of its wrapping, takes a bite or two.* **Josh** *stirs noisily in his sleep and shifts in the chair.* **Winnie** *realizes guiltily she is eating his sandwich.* **Josh** *slumbers on.* **Winnie** *carefully puts the half-eaten sandwich back in its wrapping. She attempts to start reading her book again but after a second or two, gives up. She returns to her notebook and writes a little more.* **Josh**'s *snoring gets louder causing* **Winnie** *to frown. No longer able to concentrate on her task, she gathers up her things and, leaving the half-eaten sandwich on the table in its wrapper, tip-toes out of the kitchen past the noisy* **Josh**.

3.15 p.m.

As we follow **Winnie** *back into the hall, the lights follow her. Out here, daylight is fading and the room is darker in contrast with the brightness of the kichen.* **Josh**'s *snoring fades. He remains, now unlit, in the kitchen chair.*

Winnie *moves initially to the office door but hears* **Tiffany** *crying in there and draws away and goes to the sofa and sits on it. She springs up smartly and suspiciously examines the cushion feeling it tentatively. It is apparently damp. She seats herself well away from this damp patch at the extreme other end. She places her be-*

longings on the coffee table and sets up camp again. She makes to resume her writing but has difficulty in seeing properly because of the fading light. As she is debating whether to be daring and switch the lights on, from the office the sound of **Tiffany** *crying, then the* **Man**'s *voice soothing her.*

Man. *(off)* … Tiffy, come on, come on darling. It's not the end of the world, is it?

Tiffany. *(off, tearfully)* It's all my fault. I've ruined everything for you … You should never have met me …

Man. *(off)* … it's never your fault, darling. How the hell can it be your fault …?

Tiffany *and the* **Man** *come into the office doorway, she retreating from him. A patch of light spills from the room behind them through the half-open door.*

Neither notice **Winnie** *in the gloom, absorbed as they are with each other. The following is all but whispered between the two.* **Winnie**, *whilst making no attempt to hide, instinctively draws back slightly into the sofa.*

Tiffany. *(quietly)* … it's all my fault. I should never … I'm so sorry …

Man. *(quietly)* … Tiffy …

Tiffany. *(burying her head in his shoulder)* … I'm sorry! I'm so, so sorry …

Man. *(holding her, cooing)* Tiffy! I keep saying, if it's anybody's fault, it's hers. It's Paula's. She was the one that caused it, darling. It's all Paula. She's a vindictive bitch …

Tiffany. It'll be all round the office now, won't it …?

Man. Well … What the hell! I can live with that, if you can …

Tiffany. It'll probably be all over the internet as well … we'll be on Facebook.

Man *(stroking her)* Probably. Come on, Tiffy, come here, girl …

Tiffany. Mmmm!

Man. That's good, isn't it?

Tiffany. *(wriggling from his grasp)* No, Kev! We can't, not now.

Man. Why not? She's long gone. Paula's long gone, darling. She won't be back. Come on then, upstairs, come on, Tiffy …

Tiffany. You sure?

Man. 'Course I'm sure. I love you, don't I, darling? You know I love you. Come on, this way …

The **Man** *draws* **Tiffany** *gently across the hall and towards the stairs. Neither notice the seemingly invisible* **Winnie** *on the sofa.*

(*As they do so, as if to a child*) Come on then, little Tiffy, this way. That's it …

Tiffany. *(in little girl mode, still a little tearful)* I love you, Big Bear …

Man. I love you, too, darling. Big Bear loves Ickle Tiffy, you know he does …

Tiffany. Ickle Tiffy loves Big Bear, too …

Man. *(drawing her up the stairs)* … 'course she does … Big Bear's here to look after his Ickle Tiffy you know he is … You know that, don't you?

Tiffany. *(in a baby voice)* …yeth …

Man. Ickle Tiffy's special. She's a very special Ickle Tiffy, isn't she?

Tiffany. Yeth.

Man. Anything happens to Ickle Tiffy, Big Bear would cwy and cwy …

Tiffany. *(giggling)* …yeth …

Man. He'd get cwoss. Good girl, that's it, mind the stair now — come on, Ickle Tiffy, nearly there … Big Bear will kiss it all better, won't he …?

Tiffany. … yeth, he will …

The two go upstairs.

Winnie *watches them disbelievingly as they go. Soon, when she's certain they've gone, she gropes in her schoolbag and finds another of her chocolate bars which she opens and sits munching happily. She seems unaffected and altogether unconcerned by the previous events. She considers starting to write again but realizes it is now even darker. Enterprisingly, she moves into the crack of brighter light in the office's half-open doorway, holding up her exercise book and starts to write again, eating as she does so.*

3.30 p.m.

After a moment, **Paula** *enters silently through the front door. She is an elegant, well-groomed woman in her late thirties, dressed in a dark business suit. She switches on the hall lights.*

Winnie *jumps guiltily.*

Paula. *(sharply)* Who the hell are you?

Winnie *looks up startled. We haven't seen* Paula *before but* **Winnie** *has and recognizes her from the DVD. She gapes.*

What are you doing here?

Paula *approaches* **Winnie**, *examining her more closely.* **Winnie** *nervously retreats.*

(*remembering*) Oh, yes, of course. You're Mrs Barnstairs daughter, aren't you? What's your name? It's Winnie, isn't it? Winnie Barnstairs, yes?

Winnie *nods nervously. Eventually she retreats to the safety of the sofa where she resumes her original seat.*

Your mother isn't still here, is she? She should have gone hours ago, surely? Don't tell me she's still here, it's getting on for four o'clock. What time did she come, for God's sake? Winnie, what time did you get here? What time did you arrive, you and your mother?

Winnie. *(nervously)* Nous sommes arrivés à huit trente ce matin, Madame Tate.

Paula. *(somewhat startled)* I beg your pardon?

Winnie. …à huit trente ce matin …

Paula. Eight-thirty? What on earth's she been doing all this time? Where is she?

Winnie. Je ne sais pas, Madame Tate.

Paula. Well, I'm certainly not paying her for all these hours. Costs us a fortune as it is. Where is she? Is she upstairs?

Winnie. *(squeaking)* Non! Elle n'est pas en haut!

Paula. Why are you talking in French all the time? Pourquoi parlez-vous en français?

Winnie. Parce que ma mère veut que je pratique mon français, madame.

Paula. Oh, I see. Excellent. Good for Mrs Barnstairs. Wish my wretched mother'd made me practise French instead of packing me off on a cookery course. Far more use. Is my husband here? Est-il mon mari ici?

Winnie. *(shrugging)* C'est possible, Madame Tate.

Paula. *(amused)* Well, you are a shy little thing, aren't you? What are you so nervous about? You don't need to be frightened of me, you know? I'm very fond of children. Unlike my husband. Children seem to bring him out in a rash for some reason, whenever the topic is raised.

She sits beside **Winnie** *on the damp patch of which she seems initially unaware. During the next, as she speaks,* **Winnie** *searches in her bag for her French dictionary.*

(Gently, but rapidly) Je suis fanatique des enfants. Il n'y a aucun besoin d'avoir peur de moi, Winnie. J'aimerais avoir des enfants de mes propres. Rien ne me rendrait plus heureux. Seulment mon mari ne les aime pas. Mais j'aimerais avoir une petite fille comme toi, Winnie. Tristement il obtient peu un en retard dans ma vie pour le tout cela — vous me comprenez?

Winnie. *(clutching her dictionary)* Non, madame. Je ne parle pas français vite ——

Paula. *(patiently, slower)* J'ai dit que j'étais fanatique des enfants et je … *(becoming aware that she is sitting on something damp and jumping up)* God, what's happened here? What the hell has happened to my sofa? *(She examines the cushion.)* It's soaking wet! It's soaked! What have you spilt on here? Have you spilt your drink on here, you little horror? Do you know how much this sofa cost me? Have you any idea?

Winnie. Non, madame …

Paula. It's ruined, absolutely ruined, you realize that? What is this you've spilt on it? *(examining the fabric more carefully, sniffing)* Christ, it's smells like pee. Have you been pee-ing on my sofa, you horrendous creature?

Winnie. *(terrified)* Non, madame, ce n'est pas pee …

Paula. *(fiercely)* Then who did, if it wasn't you? Tell me how this piss got on my sofa. Come on!

Winnie. Ma mère … elle … ma mère, elle est … *(She searches her dictionary for the word.)*

Paula. Your mother? Don't tell me your mother peed on the sofa, because, I don't believe you …

Winnie. Ma mère était — *(finding the word)* — était — enceinte … enceinte …

Paula. Enceinte? Yes, I know she's pregnant, you stupid girl …

Winnie. … et elle entrée dans le travail. Et ses eaux s'est cassée …

Paula. *(fiercely)* What? What the hell are you talking about?

Winnie. *(excitedly)* … le cascade … tout à coup! Comme ça! Deluge! Sur le couche! Soudainement! *(She gives up on her French and tosses the dictionary aside. Rapidly, yelling.)* My mother's waters broke and she came and went all over your sofa!

Paula. *(digesting this)* Your mother … came … and went … on my sofa?

Winnie. *(quietly)* Oui, madame. C'est vrai.

Paula. *(immediately penitent)* Oh, dear God, you poor child. You poor, poor child! What an ordeal! *(staring intently into* **Winnie***'s eyes)* Winnie, I apologize. I am so sorry. Will you forgive me? *(pausing to gather her composure)* Ever since I was your age, I've had this appalling temper. My mother used to say to me, Paula, when you grow up if you carry on with that temper of yours, my dear, by the end of your life, no one's going to bother to turn up for your funeral. You'll be lying there all alone in that crematorium with only yourself to blame. It's unforgivable. I fly into these blind rages and then I say things … I hurt people. I lose them as friends, I lose them as … Now I've gone and shouted at you which is unforgivable. *(dramatically)* God, you're a mere child! I've started shouting at kids! He's right! I'm a monster! Here you were sitting peacefully, innocently writing your little story … and I march in, jumping to all the wrong conclusions … bellowing and screaming …

Paula, *in a fit of contrition, embraces* **Winnie**.

(holding her tightly) Forgive me, darling? Please forgive me?

Winnie. *(slightly muffled)* Oui, Madame Tate.

Paula. God never forgives us, you know, any of us, if we harm a child.

Paula *kisses the top of* **Winnie** *'s head.*

(*holding her at arm's length*) Winnie, you are to bear witness. You have seen the very last of my childlish, thoughtless tantrums. No more of them, my darling. I promise. From now on, I vow, I solemnly promise. (*more briskly, her business self taking over*) Now, then, Winnie. What time did your mother go into hospital? Was she taken in an ambulance? I hope my husband had the sense to phone for an ambulance?

Winnie. Oui, madame.

Paula. What time did they take her in, do you know?

Winnie. Peu après douze heures, madame.

Paula. (*glancing at her watch*) What time is it now? One — two — three … Well, in a minute or two, I'll drive you up there, shall I? We can check how she's getting on.

Winnie. Merci, madame.

Paula. Where's Mr Tate, do you know?

Winnie. (*evasively*) Non.

Paula. Is he here?

Winnie *shrugs.*

He's not here?

Winnie *shrugs again.*

Did he go with your mother in the ambulance? No, he'd hardly leave you here all alone, would he? Where is he?

Winnie. Je ne sais pas, madame.

Paula. Well, I'll tell you what, let's go on a hunt for him, shall we? You want to come with me on a hunt for Mr Tate?

Paula *grabs* **Winnie** *'s hand before she can protest.*

Off we go. Where shall we start? Shall we start in the kitchen? Let's see if he's in the kitchen, shall we? Tippy-toes now, so we can surprise him …Tippy-toes …

Paula leads Winnie through to the kitchen. The lights come up on Josh who is still asleep, snoring gently as they enter.

Oh, no! What the hell's he doing here? Josh! Josh, wake up!

Josh. *(waking up with a start)* Wah! *(His alarm bells immediately starting to ring.)* Oh, my God! Paula!

Paula. What are you doing here Josh, for God's sake?

Josh. *(still half asleep)* I just ... I just ... looked in ... was passing through, you know ... sort of thing ...

Paula. Have you seen Kevin? Do you know where he is?

Josh. He's — he's ... I don't know, Paula ... I don't know if he's even here ... He's not even here.

Paula. But he let you in?

Josh. Oh, yes.

Paula. He's somewhere in the house then?

Josh notices the sandwich packet which is still on the table where Winnie left it.

Josh. *(opening it now)* Oh, yes. He's — he's — he's probably — somewhere — in the house ...

He is holding the half-eaten sandwich that Winnie replaced earlier. He stares at it puzzled. He looks at Winnie who avoids his look.

Paula. Right, let's go and find him. Come along, Winnie. Let's look in the office.

Paula leads Winnie out of the kitchen and back into the hall. Josh hurries ahead of them them.

Josh. *(intercepting them)* No, no, Paula, you don't want to look in the office. He won't want to be disturbed. Kev said he was specially busy and no one was to disturb him.

Paula. That doesn't include me.

Josh. *(barring the office doorway)* Just a tick then, just a tick! *(calling through the still half-open door)* Excuse me! Kevin! Kevin, mate! Bit of a surprise for you here, mate. Paula's popped back. *(He listens.)* Kev! *(He peers inside the office, cautiously. With a shade of relief.)* No, he's not in there.

Paula. *(smiling)* Apparently not.

Josh. They must have gone out for lunch. He. Must have. Gone out. To lunch.

Silence.

Paula. They?
Josh. They?
Paula. You said they? Who's they?
Josh. Kev — and — her mother.
Paula. Her mother?
Josh. Yes.
Paula. Winnie's mother?
Josh. That's right. You know. He thought he'd treat her. Sort of — thank you.
Paula. By taking Mrs Barnstairs out to lunch?
Josh. S'right.
Paula. How lovely. They're both dining in the maternity ward, I take it?

Silence.

Josh. *(coming clean)* I've no idea where he is, Paula. Unless he's upstairs having a lie down. He was a bit tired earlier. Yes. That's probably it. He's maybe having a kip. Don't want to disturb his kip, do we?
Paula. *(dangerously)* Tell you what, we'll have a look up there then, shall we, Winnie? To see if Mr Tate's hiding upstairs. Perhaps he's crouching in a cupboard without his trousers on, you never know, waiting to jump out at us and shout "Boo". Let's go up and see if we can surprise him first, shall we? Then we can shout "BOO!" at him. Come on, come with me.
Winnie. *(pulling away from Paula's grasp)* Non, non, madame! Je ne veux pas monter là!
Paula. What's the matter, Winnie?
Winnie. Non! Ma mère n'approuverait pas. Je ne dois pas voir des choses comme cela! Je suis trop jeune!

Paula *stares at* **Winnie.**

Josh. *(apprehensively)* What did she say?
Paula. *(grimly)* Enough. She said quite enough. Wait there, Winnie.
Josh. *(moving forward)* Paula!
Paula. *(steely)* Both of you! *(To Winnie, pointing fiercely)* Attente là!

Paula *goes upstairs.*

Josh. *(softly, to* **Winnie***)* Are they really up there?
Winnie. Oui, monsieur.
Josh. What, both of them?
Winnie. Yes!
Josh. Oh, Jesus!

Josh *hurtles up the stairs after* **Paula***.*

(*as he goes*) KEV!!!

Winnie *remains watching in the hall.*

A succession of noises from upstairs. First, a blood-curdling bellow of rage from **Paula***. A cry of pain from the* **Man** *cut off abruptly by a sickening thud. A scream of terror from* **Tiffany***. Ineffectual noises from* **Josh** *vainly trying to calm the situation.*

In a second, **Tiffany** *comes rushing downstairs, whimpering with terror. She has a sheet wrapped round her but appears to be wearing precious little else. Pursuing her, close behind, is* **Paula***, holding* **Tiffany***'s bundle of clothes.* **Tiffany** *reaches the hall and scampers like a terrified rabbit this way and that, as* **Paula** *grimly closes on her.*

Winnie *scuttles back to her seat on the sofa.*

Paula. *(pursuing* **Tiffany***)* Come here, you greasy slut ... you dumpy bitch... you hussy, you shameless little whore ... you cheap tramp ... you podgy strumpet ... you pathetic, half-baked tart ...
Tiffany. *(evading her, whimpering with fear)* ... no, please, please don't ... I didn't mean any harm ... please don't hurt me ... please ...

Tiffany *is finally forced to retreat through the front door.*

(*Off*) ... no ... not out here in the road. I need my clothes, let me get dressed first, please!
Paula. You get dressed in the street where you belong, you brainless little bimbo!

Paula *follows* **Tiffany** *out and throws the clothes after her.*

(*Off*) And stay out!

The sound of the front door slamming.

> **Paula** *marches back to the stairs again. She is now clutching* **Tiffany**'s *sheet.*

> (*muttering as she goes*) And don't you ever set foot in my bloody house again!

> **Paula** *goes off upstairs, ignoring* **Winnie** *who once again appears to have been forgotten.*

Winnie *is sitting quietly. She takes up her exercise book once more and writes.*

Through the letter box, **Tiffany**'s *voice is heard pleading.*

Tiffany.   (*off, slightly muffled*) Could someone let me in again, please …? Somebody? … Please! … It's freezing cold out here … (*Her teeth chattering.*) I've got no clothes on … Nothing at all …

Winnie, *considering whether to help her, rises tentatively.*

> (*Off, giving it her last shot, in her baby voice again*) Ickle Tiffy's out here in the cold!

On hearing this, **Winnie** *re-considers, scowls and promptly sits down again.*

> (*Off*) … please … anybody? … Somebody help Ickle Tiffy … please! (*after a slight pause, giving up, in her normal voice*) Oh, Jesus! Let me in, you fucking bastards! (*pause, then seeing something*) Oh. I say! I say! Over here, please! Taxi! TAXI!

A squeal of brakes outside as the taxi does an emergency stop.

> *The* **Man** *clasping a cold flannel to his forehead, comes uncertainly downstairs supported by* **Josh**. *There is evidence of some blood.* **Paula** *follows them, a pace or two behind. Her manner is now slightly more subdued.*

Man. *(in pain)* Oh, God!

Josh. *(guiding him down the stairs)* All right, easy, Kev, easy. Careful! There you go. Steady!

Man. My head! It's killing me!

Josh. Yes, it looked fairly deep, mate, you ought to get that looked at, Kev. It's a nasty gash ——

Paula. *(muttering)* Good.

Josh. What did you hit him with? What did she hit you with, for God's sake?

Man. With her BAFTA. She hit me with her sodding BAFTA.

Paula. *(drily)* Came in useful for something.

They process to the front door.

Josh. You may need a stitch or two. Probably not too serious.

Paula. Pity.

Josh. I'll run you up to A&E. I'll drive. Don't worry. I'll drive. We'll go in mine, Kev.

Man. So long as she's not driving, I don't care. Just don't let her drive, will you? I don't even want her in the same car!

Josh. No way … It's all right. All right. I'm driving.

They go out.

(*As they go*) You'll have to give me a hand with him, Paula, just getting him in.

Paula. *(off)* If I have to …

Josh. *(off)* Just watch his head as he gets in …

Winnie *is alone again, still sitting on the sofa writing in her exercise book. She seems perfectly happy. A car starts up outside and drives off.*

5.00 p.m.

Paula *comes back through the front door.*

Winnie *looks up.*

Paula. Thought I'd forgotten about you, didn't you? Come on, I promised I'd take you up to the hospital, didn't I? To see your mum? Bring your things.

Winnie. *(gathering up her stuff)* Oui, madame. Merci beaucoup, madame.

Winnie *eagerly packs up.*

Paula. *(watching her, ruefully)* I'm afraid I broke my promise to you, didn't I? Lost my temper again. It's still not good to lose your temper but it's sometimes very, very difficult you'll find, Winnie. Especially if you go and marry a berk like that. Come on, love. *(holding out her hand)* Off we go. Nous nous voyagerons ensemble dans ma voiture. Oui? C'est bon?

They go out hand in hand.

Winnie. *(as they go)* C'est bon, madame. C'est très bon. Merci beaucoup.

A quick montage of appropriate sounds and a lighting change to a hospital room.

Paula *and* **Winnie** *remain onstage.*

Laverne *is wheeled on in a hospital bed.*

Paula, *still holding* **Winnie**'s *hand, enters this new room.*

5.30 p.m.

Paula There she is! There's Mummy. There's your mum. We've found her at last!

Laverne *(rather weakly, happily)* Darling!

Winnie *silently runs to hug her mother.* **Laverne** *strokes her daughter's head.*

Here she is! Here's my darling! Thank you so much, Mrs Tate. I hope she's not been too much trouble to you.

Paula. She's been as good as gold, haven't you, Winnie?

Laverne. I got really worried about you, darling, I really did.

Paula. She's been fine. And they've just let us have a little peep at the baby. We had a look through the window just now, didn't we, Winnie? A quick peep at baby Barnstairs. He's gorgeous! Has he got a name yet?

Laverne. Oh, yes. We're calling him Jericho.

Still clinging to her mother, **Winnie** *gives a muffled groan.*

Paula. Jericho?

Laverne. Jericho. Alexander. Samson.

Paula. *(taking this in)* Great. Fine. That should keep him out of trouble, shouldn't it? Well, I won't — hang about — leave you two — I must just go and — visit — another patient. Switch off his life support. Take care. See you soon. Au 'voir, Winnie.

Winnie. Au 'voir, Madame Tate.

Laverne. Bye-bye. Thanks again, Mrs Tate. Thank you for bringing her.

    Paula *goes.*

Laverne. Oh, he's a little beauty. You've got a lovely baby brother, Winnie. Isn't that nice. God's been good.

Winnie. Does he have to be called Jericho?

Laverne. I like Jericho. It's strong. Good for a boy. Don't you like it?

Winnie. No, I hate it. It's a stupid name, Mum. Everyone'll laugh at him.

Laverne. They won't!

Winnie. They will!

Laverne. Oh. What do you think we should call him, then?

Winnie. I don't know.

Laverne. Well. *(She considers.)* How about we call him after Mr. Tate then? We could call him Kevin, couldn't we, after Mr. Tate. Seeing they've both been so kind to us. She'd appreciate that as well. What do you think, Winnie? Shall we call him Kevin?

Winnie. *(immediately)* Jericho.

Laverne. Jericho?

Winnie. Jericho.

Laverne. Jericho it is. Now, I hope you've been good and well behaved today, Winnie. Been practising your French, like you promised me?

Winnie Yes.

Laverne What?

Winnie Oui, maman.

Laverne That's better. You keep practising now, won't you? It won't be long Winnie, darling, I promise you. We'll be climbing aboard that great big plane, flying off into the sunshine. Eh? Any day now.

Winnie *is silent.*

(*smiling*) Any day now.

Winnie. *(rather restless)* Can we go home now please, Mum?

Laverne. Not just this minute, darling.

Winnie. Soon.

Laverne. Mummy's just a little bit tired. They may need to keep her in overnight. Little Jericho was in such a hurry to come out, you see, he was that keen to see you. You can stay here. Sit with me for a little while longer.

Pause.

Have you finished your essay yet for Mrs Crackle?

Winnie *nods.*

Good girl. You can give it to her in the morning then, can't you?

Slight pause. **Winnie** *fidgets in the chair.*

Tell you what? Why don't we do like we said this morning? You could read it to me, how about that? Then I'll be able to hear all about your day, won't I? Your wonderful day. Wouldn't that be nice? Would you like to read it to Mummy, would you, darling?

Winnie *produces her exercise book.*

All right. Off we go, then.

Winnie *hesitates, uncertain whether her mother is ready for this. She sits on the bed.*

(*gently encouraging*) Come on, Winnie. I'm listening, darling. I'm all ears.

Winnie. *(reading)* "My Wonderful Day by Winnie Barnstairs. At eight o'clock my mum and I caught the bus to Mr Tate's house. Mum cleans it usually every Wednesday only today we had to come on Tuesday because my mum is expecting a baby and has to go to the clinic for a check up on the Wednesday. When I woke up I wasn't feeling very well and my mum said I needn't go to school but to go with her instead. And when we got to Mr Tate's house we rang the bell and Mr Tate let us in. He was dressed in his dressing gown and no pyjamas and his bare feet even though it was half-past eight and he seemed rather cross and I saw that he needed to cut his toe nails."

Music starts under.

"And Mum told me to sit on the sofa in the hall and to be quiet and to talk in French because we were soon going to be going off to Martinique, only I think she sometimes says this only because she is unhappy what with my dad leaving us …"

As the music builds, **Winnie** *continues reading silently.* **Laverne** *lies back, initially smiling proudly as she listens to her child's detailed account of her day. As* **Winnie** *silently continues,* **Laverne** *starts to frown, eventually snatching the exercise book from her daughter and starting to read it for herself, with an expression of growing consternation. She continues to read giving* **Winnie** *the occasional incredulous glance as the music continues and the lights fade to —*

BLACK-OUT

Also by
Alan Ayckbourn...

Absurd Person Singular
Awaking Beauty (music by
   Denis King)
Bedroom Farce
Body Language
Callisto 5
The Champion of Paribanou
A Chorus of Disapproval
Comic Potential
Communicating Doors
Confusions
A Cut in the Rates
Damsels in Distress (trilogy:
   FlatSpin, GamePlan, Role-
   Play)
Dreams from a Summer House
   (music by John Pattison)
Drowning on Dry Land
Ernie's Incredible Illucinations
Family Circles
Garden
Gizmo
Henceforward ...
House
House & Garden
How the Other Half Loves
If I Were You
Improbable Fiction (music by
   Denis King)
Intimate Exchanges (Volume I)
Intimate Exchanges (Volume II)
Invisible Friends
It Could Be Any One of Us
Joking Apart
Just Between Ourselves
Life and Beth

Living Together
Man of the Moment
Mixed Doubles
Mr A's Amazing Maze Plays
Mr Whatnot
My Very Own Story
The Norman Conquests
Orvin — Champion of Champi-
   ons (music by Denis King)
Relatively Speaking
The Revengers' Comedies
Round and Round the Garden
Season's Greetings
Sisterly Feelings
A Small Family Business
Snake in the Grass
Suburban Strains (music by
   Paul Todd)
Table Manners
Taking Steps
Ten Times Table
Things We Do For Love
This Is Where We Came In
Time and Time Again
Time of My Life
Tons of Money (revised version)
Way Upstream
Whenever (music by Denis
   King)
Wildest Dreams
Wolf at the Door (adapted from
   Henri Becque's Les Cor-
   beaux)
Woman in Mind
A Word from Our Sponsor
   (music by John Pattison)

OTHER TITLES AVAILABLE FROM SAMUEL FRENCH

THE NORMAN CONQUESTS

Alan Ayckbourn

Full Length, Comedies

Winner! - Tony Award Best Revival of a Play, 2009

Winner! - Outer Critics Circle Outstanding Revival of a Play, 2009

Living Together, Round and Round the Garden and *Table Manners* make up this trilogy of plays. All occur during a single weekend in different parts of the same house and concern a group of related people. Each is complete in itself and can be played alone, or as a group they can be performed in any order. However, each benefits when produced with the others. A common factor is Norman's inadequate attempts to involve himself in turn with his sister in law, his brother in law's wife and his own wife. See individual play descriptions below.

"To write one brilliant comedy is a feat. To write three in a row is a tour de force so exceptional I can only throw my hat in the air and rejoice."
– *London Daily Telegraph*

9 780573 699498